IMAGINE

Alison Lester

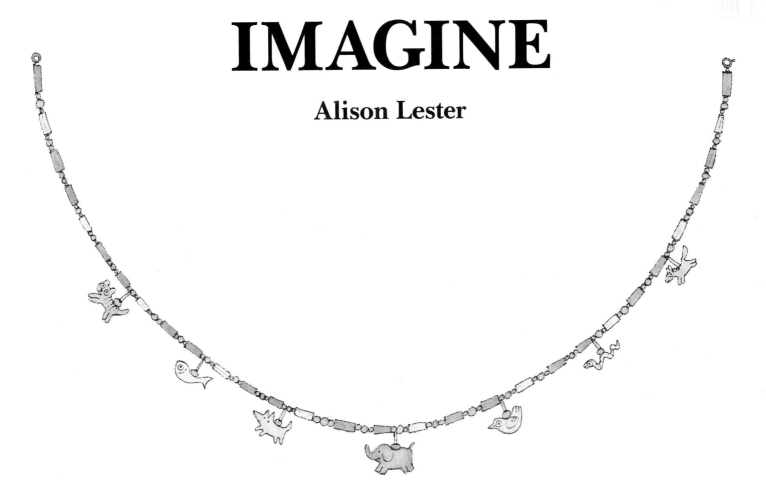

For Rich and Bee

ALLEN&UNWIN

Imagine
if we were
deep in the jungle
where butterflies drift
and jaguars prowl
where parakeets squawk
and wild monkeys howl . . .

■

cutter ant • harpy eagle • vampire bat • marsh deer • cock-of-the-rock • giant anteater • ocelot • murine opossum • tamandua • tapir • fresh-water dolphin • porcupine • giant armadillo • scarlet ibis • bird-eating spider • butterfly • macaw • jaguar • leaf-cutter ant • tapir

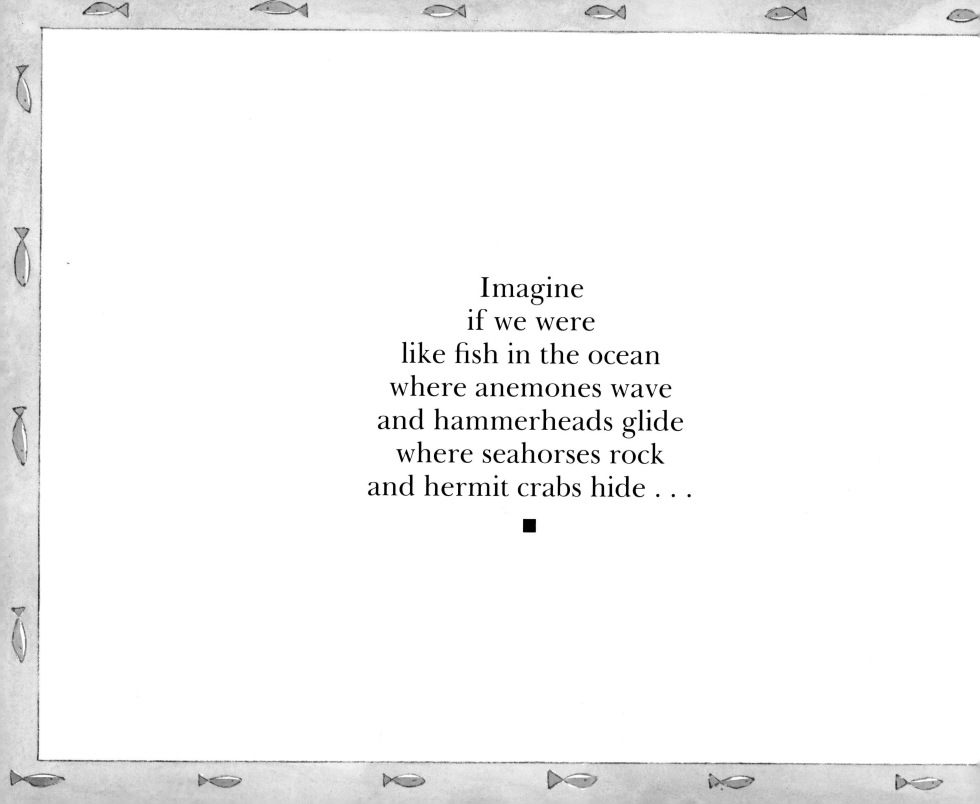

Imagine
if we were
like fish in the ocean
where anemones wave
and hammerheads glide
where seahorses rock
and hermit crabs hide . . .

■

le • hermit crab • sawfish • butterfly fish • giant clam • angelfish • angler fish • sea-snake • sponge •

tusk fish • hammerhead shark • prawn • starfish • moray eel • stingray

ving fish • trumpet-fish • swordfish • flounder • moorish idol • limpet • clownfish • anemone • oyster •

Imagine
if we were
crossing the icecap
where penguins toboggan
and arctic hares dash
where caribou snort
and killer whales crash . . .

■

• arctic squirrel • walrus • harp seal • guillemot • kittiwake • herring • polar bear • beluga whale •

killer whale • humpback whale • narwhal • arctic dolphin • arctic hare

mpback whale • narwhal • arctic dolphin • husky •adelie penguin• snowy owl • arctic squirrel • loon •

Imagine
if we were
out in the country
where horses gallop
and cattle graze
where turkeys gobble
and sheepdogs laze . . .

■

bull • cow • calf • cat • kitten • stockhorse • foal • pony • draughthorse • sheepdog • puppy • sheep •

foal • pig • goat • cockatoo • swan • cat • calf • piglet • drake • sheep • turkey

• cockatoo • goat • draughthorse • sheepdog • puppy • sheep • drake • duckling • rabbit • pig • roo

Imagine
if we were
surrounded by monsters
where pteranodons swoop
and triceratops smash
where stegosaurs stomp
and tyrannosaurs gnash . . .

∎

monoclonius • brontosaurus • ankylosaurus • dimetrodon • protoceratops • deinonychus • tyra

brontosaurus • ankylosaurus • dimetrodon • protoceratops • deinonychus

parasaurolophus • iguanodon • woolly mammoth • pteranodon • corythosaurus • diplodocus

Imagine
if we were
away on safari
where crocodiles lurk
and antelope feed
where leopards attack
and zebras stampede . . .

■

n • crocodile • rhinoceros • colobus monkey • warthog • zebra • jackal • baboon • ibex • impala •

aardvark • flamingo • vulture • crowned crane • leopard • okapi • dik-dik

pi • dik-dik • chimpanzee • gazelle • ostrich • leopard • bushbaby • buffalo • elephant • cheetah

Imagine
if we were
alone in the moonlight
where bandicoots nibble
and wallabies jump
where wombats dig burrows
and kangaroos thump . . .

■

ypus • lyrebird • tasmanian tiger • flying fox • tawny frogmouth • cockatoo • koala • tiger quoll

ringtail possum • sugar glider • wombat • bandicoot • marsupial mouse

m • flying fox • bandicoot • tiger quoll • sugar glider • tasmanian tiger • tawny frogmouth • emu

Imagine
if we had
our own little house
with a cat on the bed
a rug on the floor
a light in the night
and a dog at the door . . .

∎

Imagine . . .

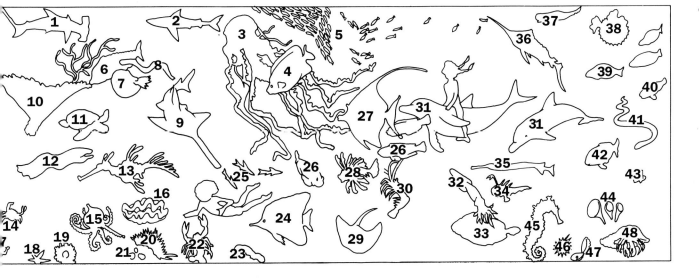

KEY

JUNGLE

1	anaconda	17	leaf-cutter ant
2	three-toed sloth	18	tamandua
3	butterfly	19	howler monkey
4	harpy eagle	20	spider monkey
5	vampire bat	21	bird-eating spider
6	toucan	22	boa constrictor
7	macaw	23	tapir
8	marsh deer	24	freshwater dolphin
9	cock-of-the-rock	25	twist-necked turtle
10	tree frog	26	water cavy
11	paca	27	piranha
12	jaguar	28	cayman
13	giant anteater	29	peccary
14	murine opossum	30	porcupine
15	ocelot	31	giant armadillo
16	hummingbird	32	scarlet ibis

OCEAN

1	hammerhead shark	25	flying fish
2	white pointer shark	26	parrot fish
3	jellyfish	27	moorish idol
4	angelfish	28	scorpion-fish
5	mullet	29	stingray
6	snapper	30	prawn
7	nautilus	31	dolphin
8	lamprey	32	squid
9	sawfish	33	flounder
10	coral	34	angler fish
11	turtle	35	trumpet fish
12	moray eel	36	swordfish
13	sea-dragon	37	sperm whale
14	crab	38	puffer fish
15	octopus	39	wrasse
16	giant clam	40	clownfish
17	cowrie	41	sea-snake
18	starfish	42	tusk fish
19	anemone	43	scallop
20	nudibranch	44	sponge
21	limpet	45	seahorse
22	lobster	46	sea-urchin
23	sea-cucumber	47	oyster
24	butterfly fish	48	hermit crab

ICECAP

1	musk ox	15	herring
2	arctic wolf	16	beluga whale
3	guillemot	17	albatross
4	sea lion	18	adelie penguin
5	arctic dolphin	19	harp seal
6	arctic tern	20	snow goose
7	polar bear	21	kittiwake
8	loon	22	caribou
9	arctic hare	23	humpback whale
10	emperor penguin	24	killer whale
11	puffin	25	arctic squirrel
12	husky	26	snowy owl
13	narwhal	27	lemming
14	elephant seal	28	walrus

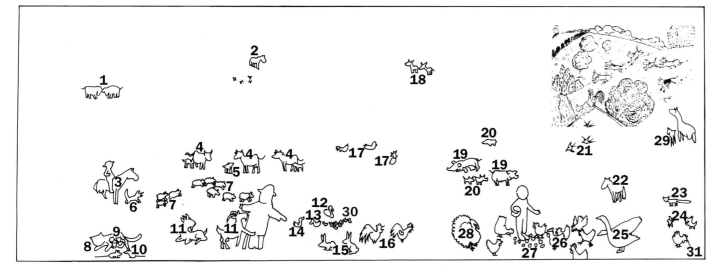

FARM

1	bull	17	cockatoo
2	draughthorse	18	donkey
3	stockhorse	19	pig
4	cow	20	piglet
5	calf	21	swallow
6	sheepdog	22	pony
7	sheep	23	fox
8	cat	24	puppy
9	kitten	25	goose
10	mouse	26	hen
11	goat	27	chick
12	swan	28	turkey
13	duck	29	foal
14	drake	30	duckling
15	rabbit	31	worm
16	rooster		

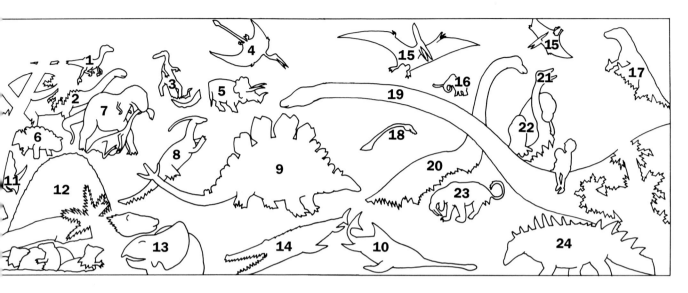

DINOSAUR SWAMP

1	deinonychus	13	protoceratops
2	brontosaurus	14	metriorhynchus
3	anatosaurus	15	pteranodon
4	rhamphorhynchus	16	woolly mammoth
5	triceratops	17	iguanodon
6	ankylosaurus	18	elasmosaurus
7	tyrannosaurus	19	diplodocus
8	parasaurolophus	20	brachiosaurus
9	stegosaurus	21	corythosaurus
10	ichthyosaurus	22	allosaurus
11	monoclonius	23	sabre-toothed tiger
12	dimetrodon	24	polacanthus

AFRICAN PLAIN

1	vulture	17	lion
2	leopard	18	zebra
3	giraffe	19	wildebeest
4	gazelle	20	impala
5	okapi	21	antelope
6	buffalo	22	elephant
7	orynx	23	dik-dik
8	ibex	24	ostrich
9	baboon	25	cheetah
10	crowned crane	26	warthog
11	hippopotamus	27	hyena
12	rhinoceros	28	chimpanzee
13	crocodile	29	bush baby
14	mandrill	30	flamingo
15	aardvark	31	colobus monkey
16	jackal	32	gorilla

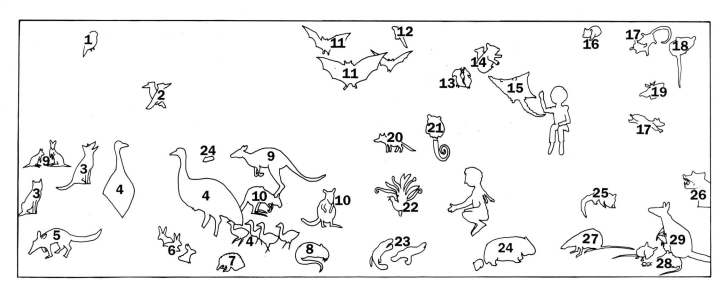

AUSTRALIAN BUSH

1	mopoke	16	tiger quoll
2	kookaburra	17	sugar glider
3	dingo	18	pigmy possum
4	emu	19	emperor gum n
5	numbat	20	tasmanian tiger
6	rabbit	21	ringtail possum
7	echidna	22	lyrebird
8	water-rat	23	platypus
9	kangaroo	24	wombat
10	wallaby	25	brushtail possun
11	flying fox	26	tasmanian devil
12	tawny frogmouth	27	bandicoot
13	cockatoo	28	marsupial mous
14	koala	29	pademelon
15	feather-tail glider		